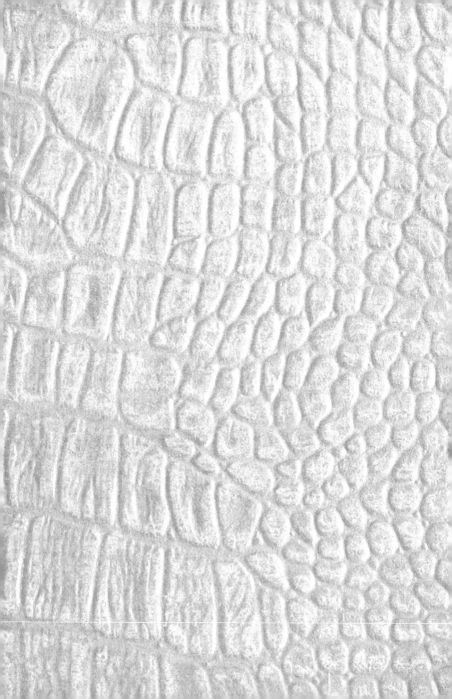

THE MYSTERY IN

ALLIGATOR ALLEY

by Carole Marsh

Published by Gallopade International/Carole Marsh Books.
Printed in the United States of America.

First Edition ©2013 Carole Marsh/Gallopade International/Peachtree City, GA
Current Edition ©2013
Ebook edition ©2013
All rights reserved.
Manufactured in Peachtree City, GA

Managing Editor: Janice Baker
Assistant Editor: Susan Walworth
Cover Design: John Hanson
Content Design: Randolyn Friedlander

Gallopade is proud to be a member and supporter of these educational organizations and associations:

American Booksellers Association
American Library Association
International Reading Association
National Association for Gifted Children
The National School Supply and Equipment Association
Museum Store Association
Association of Partners for Public Lands
Association of Booksellers for Children

Once upon a time ...

Hmm, kids keep asking me to write a mystery book. What shall I do?

Mimi

Papa said ...

Why don't you set the stories in real locations?

You sure are characters, that's all I've got to say!

Yes, you are! And, of course, I choose you! But what should I write about?

 National Parks!

 SCARY PLACES!

Famous Places!

FUN PLACES!

 Disney World!

New York City!

Dracula's Castle

GRAND CANYON

 Write one about spiders!

7

We can go on the *Mystery Girl* airplane ...

I can FLY US anywHERE!

Or aboard the *Mimi!*

Take me to the Forbidden City!

Or by surfboard, rickshaw, motorbike, camel ...!

I can put a lot of **history, MYSTERY, SCIENCE,** legend, lore, and **laughs** in the books! It will be educational and fun!

Good stuff!

And so, join Mimi, Papa, Christina, Grant, Avery, Ella, Evan, and Sadie aboard the *Mystery Girl*—where the adventure is real and so are the characters!

START YOUR ADVENTURE TODAY!

READ THE BOOK!

GO ONLINE!

TRACK YOUR ADVENTURES!

MEET THE CHARACTERS!

www.carolemarshmysteries.com

A Note from the Author

WHERE IS ALLIGATOR ALLEY?

In this story, we go to the Savannah National Wildlife Refuge on the Georgia/South Carolina border. The highway that runs through here is known as Alligator Alley!   However, if you Google "alligator alley," you will find alligator alleys all throughout the Southeast. Those gators really get around!

I am a big fan of alligators—I hope you are too! Never forget that alligators are wild animals and should never be approached. They are deserving of protection so that they will always be around.

Join us now as we go on a real life adventure with real kids as characters...to ALLIGATOR ALLEY!

— *Carole Marsh*

Range of the American Alligator

11

1

GATOR BAIT

Evan watched bubbles gurgle up from the murky water. They skimmed across the dark surface, turning slowly to display rainbows of color, before popping unexpectedly. Frustrated, he lay down his fishing pole and stretched out on the spongy ground. Mashed potato clouds were piled high on a blue plate sky. Sure, the scenery was beautiful at the Savannah National Wildlife Refuge, but Evan was disappointed. He'd been here with his cousin Christina and his sister Avery for several hours, and he hadn't even caught a fish. He had seen plenty of wildlife—wood storks, deer, ducks, and all sorts of critters, except the one he wanted to see most—an **alligator.**

Evan closed his eyes and let his imagination run wild as a wildebeest. He was holding a glistening knife between his teeth and glaring bravely into the eyes of the prehistoric-looking beast. Always the hero, he warned his sister and cousin to stay back and dove onto the scaly back of an alligator more than twice his size! The gator plunged into the water, taking Evan with him. He rolled over and over like a log. Evan was about to get the best of the **cantankerous** creature when something interrupted his daydream.

His eyes snapped open. Something had really chomped down on his earlobe! Evan jumped to his feet and flailed his arms wildly. "Help!" he screamed. "A gator's got me!"

Startled, Christina and Avery looked up from their sketchpads. Both were busy drawing a tall sandhill crane wading near the bank. Evan's commotion scared the lanky bird. It sounded like a bugler warning the other wildlife of danger before its large gray wings lifted it into the air.

Fearing her little brother was being gobbled alive, Avery slung her pad and pencil. They splashed in the water's edge. Christina jumped to her feet, ready to help her cousin fight off his vicious foe, but instead started laughing. Dangling from Evan's ear like a pirate's earring was a little green lizard.

Christina gently plucked the wriggling fellow from his ear like she was picking a pepper from a plant and placed it gently on the ground. "You gotta watch out for those gators," she said, winking at her cousin.

Evan held one hand over his pounding heart and rubbed his earlobe with the other. He quickly checked his fingers to make sure there was no blood.

"Not even a scratch," Avery said, examining her brother's ear. "The little guy probably thought you were a juicy worm lying in the grass. He only pinched you. He doesn't even have any teeth!"

Evan shuddered. "If that was a pinch, I'd hate to see what a real gator could do!"

"I hope you never get close enough to find out!" Christina said. "Alligators are serious business. You should never get anywhere near them."

Christina couldn't believe her own ears. She sounded just like her grandparents. For years, she'd gotten herself and her brother Grant into plenty of **predicaments**. They'd followed their mystery-writing grandmother Mimi and their cowboy-pilot grandfather Papa all over the world. But now she was a college student at the Savannah College of Art and Design in nearby Savannah, Georgia. Her "what they don't know won't hurt them" attitude was gone.

She remembered it was a gator encounter that had brought her here in the first place. Mimi and Papa, who'd recently moved to Palmetto Bluff, South Carolina, had already planned to have their grandkids at their new home when the accident happened. Mimi was playing a round of golf at the May River Golf Club when her ball rolled into a small pond. When she reached in to get it, she found herself ankle to eye with a small gator.

"I walked on air!" Mimi had told them. But when she came down, the impact broke her leg. Now she was home, miserable, and Papa was taking care of her. They were unable to do all the things they'd planned during the grandkids' fall school break, including taking Avery and Evan to the wildlife **refuge**. Christina was proud she could fill in, at least for the day.

KERSPLASH! The sound came from where Christina and Avery had been practicing their art. Avery saw that her sketchpad was now back on the bank. She walked over and picked up the soggy paper. *Something had taken a big bite out of it!*

Avery is excited to be part of her
grandmother's mystery adventures!

2

POACHED GATOR

"I can't believe it," Avery said, reading a note that was scrawled on the paper's jagged edge. "I didn't know gators could write!"

This is our spot, stay away!

Evan scoured the ground looking for gator tracks—either the five-toed track of the front feet or the four webbed toes of the back feet. They'd have to be tracks large enough to carry a humongous gator that could take a basketball-sized bite from a sketchpad. But Evan saw only one track in the squishy mud near the water's edge, and he knew it didn't belong to an alligator. It was the outine of a large boot!

Of course, Evan and Avery wanted to stick around to see if whatever had munched on the crane drawing would come back for seconds. But Christina insisted they had to get to the visitors' center before it closed. Besides, she had a **geometry** test on Monday and no time to get mixed up in a mystery. She'd have to leave this one to the younger kids.

Inside the visitors' center, motionless ducks were mounted as though in flight. Furry critters stared at them with fake, glassy eyes from their display boxes. Some, like the beaver family, looked cute and cuddly. Others, like the bobcat and wild boar, snarled at them angrily.

The large skull of an alligator captured Evan's attention. He took the refuge pamphlet out of his back pocket and unfolded it. Then, he carefully placed it between the teeth and pressed the top jaw down like a stapler before rolling the pamphlet back up to put in his pocket.

Before anyone could notice what he'd done, he stuck his head in the alligator's toothy grin and told Christina, "Take my picture!"

He'd just stuck out his tongue when a pretty female ranger said, "I'm Ranger Karen. Do you have any questions?" Evan's face turned redder than his earlobe had been after the lizard attack. He quickly tried to snatch his head from the skull's mouth, but the teeth caught fast in his blond hair. When he raised his head, he was wearing the skull like a football helmet!

"Now there's the shot I want!" Christina said, gleefully snapping the picture of her always silly cousin.

Avery snickered. This is what she loved about her brother. He was unpredictable, but you could always be sure he'd make you laugh.

"Please be careful!" the ranger cautioned. She gingerly untangled Evan's hair and placed the skull back on its shelf. "We don't get too many that large."

Evan's hair, combed by gator teeth, was now sticking out in every direction. "Love the gator 'do'!" Avery teased.

Evan smooshed his hair down and asked the ranger, "How large do most of the gators on the refuge get?"

"Most of the adults here average between about 8 and 12 feet long," she said. "But some of the largest alligators ever recorded have been about 15 feet long and have weighed close to half a ton!"

"A ton?" Evan asked.

"A ton is two thousand pounds," Avery explained.

"Wow! Nearly one thousand pounds of pure alligator," exclaimed Evan, proud of his quick math calculation.

Ranger Karen pointed at the skull. "This fellow here was about 14 feet long."

"What happened to the rest of him?" Evan asked.

"Sadly, he was killed years ago by poachers," she said. "He probably became a ladies' purse or a piece of luggage."

Evan knew what poached eggs were. He'd seen Mimi make them. "Are you talking about people who crack their eggs and drop them in boiling water?" he asked.

The ranger smiled sweetly. "No. Poachers are people who kill or steal animals that are not supposed to be hunted," she explained. "Years ago, there were no laws about killing alligators and they were almost hunted to **extinction**."

"I guess alligator shoes and purses were popular then," Avery said.

"Probably," Ranger Karen agreed. "Now, there are strict laws about hunting alligators. South Carolina and several other states do issue permits for alligator hunting at certain times, but each person who gets a permit can kill only one, and it must be more than four feet long."

"Good thing I'm not an alligator," Evan said. "I'd be just the right size!"

"No one would want a purse or shoes that looked like you!" Avery teased.

Ranger Karen laughed. "Laws have helped alligators make an amazing comeback," she said, "but they're still considered threatened."

Avery noticed the gun on the ranger's hip. "Are poachers still a problem?" she asked.

"I'm afraid so," Ranger Karen said.

"I know where there's a poacher!" Evan said. "I ate at a restaurant in Florida that had alligator nuggets on the menu! I told Mimi I didn't want to eat anything that could eat me!"

"There are gator farms that raise alligators for their hides and meat," Ranger Karen explained. "I'm sure that's where the restaurant got gator. Some people say it tastes just like chicken."

"Poachers hunt wild alligators, don't they?" Avery asked.

"That's right," the ranger said. "One reason alligators are still on the threatened list is to protect their cousins, the American Crocodile. That species lives in south Florida and it's on the endangered list."

"You mean someone might accidentally kill a **crocodile** because they thought it was an alligator?" Evan asked.

"Exactly," Ranger Karen answered. "It's a case of mistaken identity because they look so similar."

The ranger continued her explanation with a serious look on her face. "But it's important to understand that poachers aren't the alligator's only enemy," she added. "Their **habitat** is threatened by human development and pollution, too.

"Who knows?" she continued. "Maybe one of you will grow up and find a solution to things like pollution."

Avery, who had recently learned at school about the importance of STEM—Science, Technology, Engineering and Math—thought about the many ways science could help animals like the alligators. She was already trying to decide what she wanted to be when she grew up. "I'm thinking of becoming a **scientist!**" she told Ranger Karen.

Evan's mind was not on the future. He was thinking about the note. *Either there was a very large alligator on the refuge that could write, or they'd had a close encounter with a poacher!*

Evan is worried about the gators!

3

JEEPERS CREEPERS

Christina smiled as they walked to her red Jeep. Mimi had helped her pick it out so, of course, it had to be in her grandmother's favorite color.

Christina remembered the conversation well. "Every time you ride in it, it will be just like your Mimi's giving you a big hug," her grandmother had said.

Christina had given her an "Oh, Mimi" kind of smile and said, "Don't you think you're laying it on kind of thick?"

"OK," Mimi had admitted. "It's red enough that all those crazy college drivers in Savannah will see you coming and get out of the way."

Christina had nodded in agreement. "That's what I figured you were thinking!" she'd said.

Leaving her family and moving to college had been tough for Christina, even if she'd never admit it to anyone. There had been times during those first few weeks that she'd wondered if SCAD, as the Savannah School of Art and Design is known, was a tad more than she could handle.

She was overjoyed when her grandparents moved to Palmetto Bluff, only a few miles across the South Carolina state line from Savannah. She was an independent college woman, but if she got homesick, she could be at their house in less than an hour.

Scary as it was to be alone in a new city, Christina had fallen in love with her new hometown. She was amazed that the mossy, tree-lined historic squares in Georgia's first city still were used the same way that James Oglethorpe had designed them in the early 1700s.

When school got to be too much, she'd grab a sandwich and go sit by one of the beautiful fountains and let the sound of the gurgling water take her back in history. She'd imagine that she could see the young Mary Musgrove talking to the early Georgia settlers. Mary was the daughter of a Native American woman and an English settler. She helped the Native Americans and the settlers reach many agreements.

"Look how pretty your Jeep is!" Avery exclaimed. Leaves in every shade of buttery yellow, glistening gold, and plush purples and plums decorated the red finish like it was wearing a warm fall sweater.

It was far from cool, but Christina noticed the air felt different. The **humidity**, or water vapor in the air, that usually lay over the Lowcountry like a sopping wet blanket, had been lifted. She could tell it was easier to breathe. She usually complained that she needed gills instead of lungs to live in this part of the world.

Evan noticed the difference too. "Let's ride with the top down!" he said.

"Great idea!" Avery agreed, as she began helping Evan undo the snaps and tie that held the canvas top in place.

With the top off, they could hear the oyster-shell gravel crackling under the tires. "Keep your mouths closed!" Christina warned her passengers who had buckled themselves into the back seat. "Or you'll be picking moths out of your teeth!"

As they picked up speed, Avery's strawberry-blonde hair twirled wildly in the wind. Evan laughed when it covered her face. "Who's got messy hair now?" he asked and poked his sister.

Just as they were about to pull onto Highway 170 bound for Mimi and Papa's house, Christina slammed on the brakes. A battered truck, with maroon paint as scaly as alligator skin and a mis-matched white door on the driver's side, pulled out of the woods in front of them. It dragged a **camouflaged** boat behind it that rested uneasily on a trailer. The contraption, which was dripping wet, bounced noisily over the washboard ruts in the road.

In the fading afternoon light, Evan could make out a creepy old man wearing a camouflage cap. He looked at them in his rearview mirror. His eyes were glaring.

Evan wondered: *Could he be wearing a muddy boot?*

4

ALLIGATOR ALLEY

They followed the camo boat along the highway nicknamed Alligator Alley for the gators that sometimes lumbered across it. Evan's mind flashed back to the moonlit night long ago when he, Christina, Mimi, and Papa were speeding to Fort Sumter a couple of hours up the road in Charleston, South Carolina. Hadn't Papa swerved to miss one of the scaly rascals?

Drops of foul, fishy-smelling water showered them until the boat ahead had finally dried off. "Why don't you pass him?" Evan yelled above the wind whipping through the Jeep.

"Not safe," Christina answered with both hands firmly on the wheel at the 10:00 and 2:00 position.

"I wish we'd left the top up," Evan said, spitting out the side.

"Hey!" Christina yelled when she saw him in her rear-view mirror. "Just for that, you're washing my car!"

Evan wiped his mouth on his arm. "You really think my spit is dirtier than fish water?" he yelled.

"Smells worse!" Christina yelled back at him.

Avery enjoyed hearing their good-natured banter. She had always envied Christina's tales of mystery and adventure and hoped that one day she too could be as good at solving mysteries as Christina had always been.

CRASH! The boat trailer in front of them bounced up and came down hard. Next, it was their turn. The Jeep's tires bounced over something so large that Evan and Avery were tossed around like they were riding inside a washing machine.

"What was that?" Evan asked.

"It felt like we ran over a log," Avery said, tightening her seatbelt.

Christina gripped the steering wheel so hard her knuckles were white. "I'm not sure," she said, suddenly ready to have the kids, and herself, under the safety of Mimi and Papa's roof. "I saw something dark in the road and didn't have time to stop."

Evan and Avery turned to look at the dark stretch of road behind them.

Could it have been one of the alligators this stretch of road is famous for, Evan wondered. *Or, did a poached alligator fall out of Mr. Creepy's boat?*

5

CHRISTINA KILL-JOY

As they slowed for a stoplight, Avery remembered the technology she could use as a tool in her new role as a sleuth. Her phone had a good camera in it. She slipped it out of her pocket and quickly snapped the boat's license plate, TR 543, before the light turned green.

"Good thinking!" Evan said, nodding like he was impressed. "Never know when that might come in handy!"

A few miles later, the boat trailer's taillights flashed red and the rattletrap truck pulled off onto a narrow dirt road. "Let's follow him," Avery said. There was no doubt the mystery bug had bitten her as hard as a Lowcountry mosquito.

"No way!" Christina said sternly, surprised by her young cousin's sudden sense of adventure. "Don't you know how dangerous that would be?" Uh-oh, there she was sounding like Mimi again.

Evan and Avery exchanged a knowing look. Christina had officially become a grown-up kill-joy.

"Make a mental note of that old tree," Evan whispered to Avery. The ancient live oak had limbs that were as a gnarly as witches' fingers, and an ugly black knot that was oozing sap. "And that rusty old gate hanging on its hinges," he added. "That'll help us find this place when we come back to check it out. What Christina doesn't know won't hurt her!"

"Aren't you guys starving?" Christina asked, trying to get their minds off mystery and on their stomachs.

"Now that you mention it, I could eat my weight in some of Papa's good oyster gumbo," Evan said, but then frowned. "I only hope Mimi hasn't been trying to bake bread again today. She's a great mystery writer, but I'm afraid she still hasn't cracked the code of good homemade bread."

"Bakers need to be good at fractions and measuring," Avery said. "Without those skills, the correct chemical reactions needed to make the bread rise might not happen. Maybe Mimi just needs to brush up on her math and science skills!"

In addition to golf, baking bread was one of Mimi's many newfound hobbies since she had officially, unofficially "retired." She was also practicing her wildlife photography skills, although she'd most likely have to photograph backyard visitors for the next six weeks. She couldn't be traipsing through the woods in her cast. But living in Palmetto Bluff, a 20,000-acre island, backyard visitors could include everything from a rare bald eagle to a wild turkey, wild boar, or an everyday squirrel. An antsy armadillo, which she called an "artichoke," might even make an appearance. Mimi had told them the community had been designed with nature conservation in mind. She said people were seeing more alligators, like the one she saw on the golf course, because people had moved into the gators' territory.

We have to learn to co-exist with nature," she always said. "I want all this beauty to be around when you kids have grandkids!"

Avery knew they were getting close to Mimi and Papa's when the Jeep entered a traffic circle that threw her against the arm rest. A full moon had risen and the silver light was shining through the Spanish moss. It hung in the live oak trees like old men's gray beards.

When they pulled into the driveway, flickering gas porch lights welcomed them. Avery and Evan's siblings Ella and Sadie were peering over the porch rail like turkeys peeking over a log. Inside, Papa greeted them in his deep cowboy voice and gave each of them a bear hug like he hadn't seen them in years.

"Where are the fish?" he asked. "I can tell by the way you smell you must have caught a bushel! Need help bringing them in from the car?"

Evan looked at the floor, embarrassed by his angling skills, or more accurately, lack of skills. "There aren't any fish," he admitted. "They just weren't biting today."

"What is that smell?" Mimi said, waving one hand in the air as she hopped into the room on her good leg. With her other hand, she was steering a little cart that held her bum leg and its cast.

Evan shot Christina an annoyed look for not passing the stinky boat. "Let's just say that we got caught up in something that was fishy," he said. Evan sniffed beyond his own odor to a heavenly smell coming from the kitchen.

"Supper's ready," Papa said.

"Yes," Mimi agreed, "but I think showers are in order first. Oh, and Evan," she added, "I baked some of that homemade bread you love so much—a whole loaf just for you!"

"Oh, great," Evan said, trying to manage a weak smile. He'd have to figure out some way to get rid of that heavy, dough brick. Avery covered her mouth with her hand so Mimi wouldn't see her tickled expression.

When Evan came down after scrubbing until he smelled human again, he was surprised that the house was empty. He could hear talking and laughter outside and found everyone gobbling gumbo on the back porch beneath the twinkling globe lights Mimi had strung up, cantina-style.

Avery and Evan's sister Ella had finished her dinner and was drawing hearts with glue on Mimi's cast, then sprinkling them with red glitter. "Plain white is so boring!" she told her grandmother.

"I couldn't agree more," Mimi said, leaning back in her rocker as the young Picasso worked her magic.

Evan ladled a bowl of the steaming stew and thought how happy he was that his grandparents had moved to a place that always had fresh seafood. "Don't forget your bread!" Mimi called, as Evan poured a glass of iced tea.

He reluctantly balanced the bread on top of his bowl and walked to the picnic table in the backyard where Avery was watching her sister. Sadie was swinging like a superhero in the tire swing Papa had hung in one of the large live oaks.

Avery's mangled sketchpad was lying on the table next to her where she'd been studying it. "So, who do you think could have left this note?" Avery asked when Evan had swallowed his last spoonful of gumbo.

Avery could tell Evan was thinking, but he didn't say anything. He whistled for the family dog, Clue, broke the bread over his leg, and offered some to his four-legged pal. Clue only whimpered and tucked his tail between his legs.

"Great!" Evan said. "Now what am I going to do with this?"

"The note, Evan!" Avery said, trying to draw her brother's thoughts back to the mystery.

Evan reached in his back pocket and pulled out the refuge pamphlet he'd punched with the gator skull. He compared the cone-shaped holes to those on the sketchpad. "No doubt about it," he said. "A real gator did this. Maybe a poacher wrote it, and then the gator bit it to say, 'HELP!'"

"I'll bet our creepy camo friend knows something," Avery said.

6

LADY BUGS AND LIGHTNING BUGS

Mimi called all the kids back to the porch. She gave each of them a Mason jar. The jar lids were riddled with holes.

"What's this for?" Avery asked. "Anything you put in here is going to leak out."

Mimi smiled. "One of my favorite things to do when I was a little girl was to catch fireflies," she said.

"We called them lightning bugs back then," Papa added.

"It would cheer me up if you kids could catch some I could put in my room," Mimi said. "That way, when I turn out my lights, I can re-live those great childhood memories."

Avery had seen tiny lights twinkling in the shrubbery, but she honestly thought Papa had forgotten to take down all the Christmas decorations.

Evan ran in the house, letting the screen door SLAM! He was back in a flash with his iPad. It had been his birthday gift from Mimi and Papa and now his favorite pastime was "Googling" everything that crossed his mind. Mimi said Evan was turning into a walking encyclopedia. Papa called him an egghead.

The glowing screen turned Evan's face an eerie shade of green as his fingers worked frantically to find the information he was looking for.

"Here it is," he said. "They're actually beetles, not flies. The light comes from special organs under their abdomens. And, hey! They're like little bug scientists! They take in oxygen and mix it with something called lucy, lucy, lucy..."

Stumbling on a word he couldn't pronounce, he passed the iPad to Christina. "Luciferin," she said. "When this mixes with the oxygen, it causes a chemical reaction that makes the light."

Evan continued reading until he chuckled. "It's how they find boyfriends and girlfriends," he said. "Bet you never knew that, Mimi."

"No, I didn't," she said. "Isn't technology awesome? We had to go to the library to find out things like that when I was a little girl."

"Hey Christina," Evan said. "Maybe we should get you some of that lucy stuff so you can get a boyfriend."

Christina's cheeks glowed red. "I have to go and study."

Ella and Evan grabbed their jars and squealed with excitement. "Bet I catch more than you!" Ella told her brother. Baby Sadie, still not steady enough on her feet to chase fireflies, studied her jar with her big blue eyes. She plopped on her bottom and rolled it noisily across the wood planks of the picnic table.

Avery knew the kids were so loud that she and Evan would never catch anything. "Mind if we drive the golf cart?" she asked Papa.

Since moving to Palmetto Bluff, Papa had bought a red golf cart to drive around the paths on the island. He had a habit of naming his transportation, like his little red plane he had named *Mystery Girl*. He dubbed the golf cart *The Ladybug*."

"That's funny," Papa said while nodding yes. "You want to use a ladybug to catch fireflies!"

"Be very careful," Mimi cautioned. "This island is not Disney World. The animals that live here are wild, and dangerous!"

Evan flexed his muscles. "No worries," he boasted. "I'll be along to wrestle any wild beasts that try to bother us!"

Avery remembered how brave Evan had been during the lizard encounter and laughed. "I've got my phone," she said.

Christina, almost to the door, groaned and spun around. "Well, I'll have to drive you," she said. "You have to be at least 16 to drive a golf cart here." She knew how amazing the stars were out here in the darkness, so she really didn't mind. It was better than studying for a geometry test.

When Christina pulled *The Ladybug* around to pick up the kids, Evan said, "Wait! I've got a great idea!"

He jogged to the picnic table and tucked the bread under his arm like a football. "Drive down to the dock," he whispered. "I'll sink this bread brick like the *Titanic*. It'll be our little secret."

"Yeah," Avery said. "But when Mimi thinks you've eaten an entire loaf in one night, she'll just keep baking more!"

"You're right," Evan said. "I'll have to come up with new ways to make it disappear."

As *The Ladybug* rolled along under ancient oaks, Avery and Evan could see almost as well as if it were daylight. The moon was high and bright. It cast spooky shadows on the path.

"I'll bet there are plenty of ghosts on this island," Evan said, pointing at the massive tabby columns that had once formed the porch of a plantation mansion in the 1800s.

"Thanks for reminding me," Avery said, glancing over her shoulder. "I thought all we had to worry about were wild beasts!"

"Papa said that archie-ologists have found clay pots and stone tools here that belonged to prehistoric people," Evan continued.

"The word is **archaeologist**, Evan," Avery said. "I think it would be cool to be an ARK-E-OLOGIST," she added, emphasizing the correct pronunciation.

"Didn't you want to be a scientist this morning?" Evan asked.

"Haven't decided yet," she answered. "Besides, I'm sure they have to use a lot of science and math too."

"I'd like to be a polly-ologist," Evan said. "You know, someone who hunts and finds dinosaur bones."

"Don't you mean **paleontologist**?" Avery asked.

"Yeah, you get the *gist* of what I'm saying," Evan said, giggling at his own little joke. "Dinosaurs probably used to stomp down this very path."

"Whoa!" Avery said. "I think we need to concentrate on alligators for now."

Evan quickly pulled up a photo of an ancient alligator he'd saved on his iPad and showed it to Avery. "Alligators are like living dinosaurs," he said. "These guys have looked about the same for 180 million years!"

"I'll be honest," Avery said. "Looking at alligators gives me the willies. But I want to do everything I can to help them stay around for 180 million more years. They're not very cute or cuddly, but I know they have an important job in the **ecosystem**."

"Yep," Evan agreed. "Without them, the whole **food chain** would get out of whack. One thing could lead to another until we wouldn't have all the ingredients for gumbo! We've got to make sure no one is messing with the gators!"

At the dock, Christina mashed *The Ladybug's* parking brake until it clicked. She couldn't imagine how much trouble they'd be in if it rolled into the water. She wandered off into the dark to stare at the Milky Way, leaving the gator-crazed kids behind.

"You never know what we might see," Avery told Evan as she reached into the glove compartment and looped Mimi's bird-watching binoculars around her neck.

Crickets serenaded them with a chorus of chirps that blended into a deafening buzz as they walked to the end of the dock. The moon cast a highway of silvery light across the marshy landscape. Avery put the binoculars to her face and shivered. A long "S" shape was gliding through the water. She knew it was a snake. She also knew that some of the snakes on the island were deadly poisonous.

At least it's swimming away from us, she thought. *Unfortunately, she couldn't see the pair of dark, beady eyes watching them from the bank!*

7

BREAD BOMBS

"Awesome!" Evan yelled when the chunk of bread hit the water with an explosive SPLASH, and sank like a Savannah gray brick. "Mimi should go into the boat anchor business. She'd make a fortune with this bread!"

Evan reared his arm back to throw the second chunk, but paused when something splashed next to the dock. "Probably a bull frog," he said with a shrug. "Bombs away!" He launched the bread, but before it hit, a pair of massive jaws lunged from the water and swallowed it whole.

The kids' eyes grew as large as the full moon as they watched an armor-plated back, wide as a footbridge, floating toward the shore.

"LET'S GET OUTTA HEEEEEERE!" Evan yelled. The kids raced each other down the dock, their feet pounding the boards like thunder. Evan wasn't interested in a fair foot race with something that could eat him for supper. He wanted a good head start! But before he reached the end of the dock, Evan stumbled. Something clanked in front of him. He caught his balance and picked up the object, not stopping to see what it was.

Out of breath, the two of them dove into *The Ladybug*, and Avery floored it, forgetting she was not allowed to drive, or that they were leaving Christina behind. A golf cart does not make a good getaway car, she thought as it slowly puttered back on the path.

Evan sat on his knees and watched behind them. There was no sign of the gator. Still wide-eyed from the shock of seeing the reptilian monster, he said, "Mimi's bread saved our lives!"

"What do you mean?" Avery asked.

"That bread is so heavy, it weighed that 'ol gator's flat white belly down so much he couldn't chase us! That poor fellow will have a whopping bellyache tonight! Besides, if he had chased us, you could've gotten me killed."

"What are you talking about?" Avery asked, confused by her brother's accusation.

"You left your jar on the dock, and I almost fell when I stumbled over it," Evan said.

"Jar?" Avery asked. "What jar?"

"Your firefly jar," Evan said, holding it up. Two tiny lights blinked inside. "Hey! You already caught some fireflies. When did you do that?"

Avery looked at Evan like he had two heads. "I didn't catch any fireflies, and I never took my jar out of the golf cart. It's right back there with yours."

Evan looked in the back seat. Sure enough there were two jars—two empty jars. "Then where'd this come from?" he said. He turned the jar in his hand. It was definitely not like the one Mimi had given them. The fireflies blinked, and for a split second, Evan thought he saw something else inside.

"Let me borrow your phone," Evan said. He turned on the phone's flashlight app and shined it inside the jar. "It's a scrap of paper!"

Feeling that they were far enough from the alligator, Avery pulled off the road. "Let me see that," she said. She unscrewed the jar lid, releasing the fireflies. They seemed to blink "Thank you!" in **iridescent** Morse code as they flew into the night. Avery pulled out the rolled note and smoothed it down on the seat. It said:

Good haul tonight.
See you at the
next spot.

8

GATOR GOGGLES

The next morning (after she fussed at the kids for leaving her behind!), Christina announced she needed to get back to Savannah. She had plans to meet some friends for a study session at Leopold's Ice Cream Parlor to prepare for her big geometry test later in the week.

"You're so lucky!" Evan said. "They have the best ice cream in the world. If I knew I'd get their ice cream every time I studied, I'd be a straight A student."

"And probably very fat," Avery added.

Avery and Evan helped Christina carry her bags to the car. Evan had one that was particularly heavy. "What's in here?" he asked, already suspecting the answer. He peeked in the bag and gave Christina a **sympathetic** look. It was Mimi's bread.

"Do great on your test!" Avery told Christina. One of Avery's favorite activities was competitive cheerleading and she quickly burst into a cheer complete with hand motions. "GO Christina! You can DO it!" She ended with a cartwheel.

"Thanks for the encouragement," Christina said. "You kids be careful. Mysteries have a way of getting you into lots of trouble. Believe me. I've been there."

Evan gave her the most innocent look he could muster. "What mystery?" he asked.

"Well," Christina said, "just remember I'm only a phone call away!"

Evan and Avery waved until Christina was out of sight and walked back to the front porch. The morning was bright and clear, but Avery had one complaint. "Ugh!" she groaned, looking down at her turquoise sneakers. "My shoes are already soaked. I feel like I'm walking on sponges!"

"It's only the dew," Evan explained. "Warm air can hold more moisture than cold air. So, when the air gets cooler at night, it can't hold as much water and lays it on the ground. When the air heats back up in the daytime, it picks the moisture back up."

"I know what dew is, Evan," Avery said. "I'm just mad because I can't wear my favorite shoes today! Now, I'll have to wear the purple ones."

"Purple, smurple," Evan said. "Who cares what color your shoes are?" He knew better than to ask that question. His sister was a competitive cheerleader with lots of matching outfits—and a fashionista! Girls!

"Well, I happen to know that alligators can see in color," she said. "I also happen to think they'd like turquoise better than purple!"

Since a friend was spending the day with Mimi, Papa had promised to take Avery and Evan exploring. Feeling sorry for Evan's bad fishing luck, he told them to bring the fishing gear.

After Avery changed shoes, they climbed in Papa's black SUV. He took them on the scenic route to the village down the long, lovely drive lined with oaks dripping with

Spanish moss. Evan had researched that, too. He couldn't help explaining how the moss gets all the nutrients it needs from the air.

"That's right," Papa agreed. "But did you know Spanish moss is not really from Spain? Some people say it got its name from the Spanish settlers who thought it looked like their beards."

"Why don't you grow a beard, Papa?" Avery suggested. "It would make you look very distinguished, just like these trees!"

"I'll ask Mimi what she thinks about that," Papa said. He gave them a smile and a "thumbs-down" and the kids giggled.

They drove over several wooden bridges while Papa pointed out egrets, herons, and other wildlife that called the marshland home.

As they passed a lagoon, Avery begged Papa to stop. She had borrowed Mimi's binoculars again and saw something that deserved a closer look. The pond was covered with a tiny plant called duckweed that turned its surface chartreuse green.

"What do you see?" Evan asked.

Avery passed Evan the binoculars and pointed to what looked like a row of blackish-gray stones sticking up above the water. "Those look like **scutes**!" Evan cried.

"That's what I thought!" Avery agreed. She knew that scutes are the bony plates on the back of an alligator.

When Evan looked through the binoculars again, he could see that one of the stones had nostrils on top of it. He'd learned that an alligator's nose is on the top of its snout so it can lie in the water and still be able to breathe.

The next "stone" Evan saw had eyes with vertical, black-slit pupils. The mystery was solved! A gi-normous gator was watching them! Evan wondered if he was related to the gator that had eaten Mimi's bread. He knew alligators didn't have emotions like people, but he thought the beast's stony stare looked sad.

"Cool!" Evan said. "I just saw its inner eyelids close. They use those like goggles when they go underwater."

Sure enough, the gator **submerged** like a submarine. "It can stay underwater for an hour without air," he said.

Papa was worried the alligator might go to the bottom and walk out beside them. "We'd better 'scute' back to the truck," Papa suggested, smiling at his pun. "Alligators usually don't bother people, but we don't want to overstay our welcome."

"But he's your neighbor," Evan teased. "Hasn't he ever had you over for dinner?"

"No," Papa said. "That's one dinner party I don't want to attend! But it does remind me of a funny picture from a Hilton Head Island Packet newspaper I saw a few years ago. Someone saw an alligator on his neighbor's front porch. The gator was trying to climb on the door and he snapped a picture just as the alligator's "finger" touched the doorbell button. When he called his neighbors to warn them, he joked, 'Guess who's coming to dinner?'"

Evan and Avery laughed at Papa's story. But both of them were thinking the same thing. *If someone is poaching gators, could this one be next?*

9

CAMOUFLAGED MAIL

Papa pulled into the Palmetto Bluff Post Office, or "gossip central," as Mimi often called it. While Papa chatted with a neighbor, Avery and Evan moved to a corner to discuss things.

"Both of the notes we found have something in common," Avery told Evan.

"Yeah," he said. "Both of them mentioned 'spots.'"

"Maybe there's no mystery here at all," Avery said. "A lot of people have favorite fishing spots. And the note in the jar mentioned a good haul. Isn't that something fishermen say when they catch a lot?"

Evan stared at the ground. "I really wouldn't know," he said with a frown. "I never catch anything. Besides, that wouldn't explain your half-eaten sketchpad. I've never seen a fish that could do that."

Before Avery could offer another possible explanation, a young man burst through the post office doors. He glanced around nervously and headed straight for the stamp machine. Avery and Evan moved out of his way, but noticed he was dressed head to toe in camouflage. His boots left muddy footprints on the floor.

"Look at that," Avery whispered to Evan. "Do you see what's hanging around his neck?"

Evan gulped and nodded. A large white tooth hanging from a leather string stood out against his dark green undershirt.

The man dropped some coins into the machine, and when it spit out his stamp, he grabbed it and headed for a counter. He pulled a notepad from his shirt pocket and quickly scribbled a note. After he stuffed it into a crumpled envelope, he slapped on the stamp and dropped it in the mail slot. Avery noticed he chose the slot that was for out-of-town mail. When he burst back out the door as quickly as he'd come in, Evan and Avery rushed to the glass expecting to see Mr. Creepy's battered old truck. Instead, the young man got on a motorcycle and roared away.

An **exasperated** post office worker stopped sorting mail and ran to get a mop, muttering something under her breath about hunters. Avery knew there were a lot of hunters in the area. But how many of them wore alligator tooth necklaces?

Papa motioned to the kids that he was ready to leave. Avery glanced at the counter where the camo man had written his note. The notepad was still there! She grabbed it and stuck it in her pocket. They might have plenty of fancy technology, but Avery had a low-tech idea.

In the SUV, Avery showed Evan the notepad. It was from a hotel in nearby Bluffton. She rummaged through the pocket on the back of Papa's seat and found a pencil. Gently, she rubbed it lightly across the notepad. "Saw this in a movie once," she told Evan. Like magic, the words that camo man had written appeared.

"How'd you do that?" Evan asked.

"When he wrote his note he pressed down hard enough that it made an invisible copy on the paper underneath," Avery said. "When I rubbed the pencil across it, the graphite didn't get into the grooves the writing made, leaving the words white."

The kids read the note:

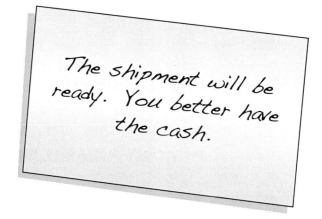

The shipment will be ready. You better have the cash.

10

EGG-CELLENT IDEA

Evan whispered questions that sounded like a machine gun as Papa's SUV rolled over the bumpity brick street. "Should we call the p-p-p-police, the r-r-r-rangers, the N-N-National Guard?"

"What would we tell them?" Avery asked. "We've got some mysterious notes?"

Avery remembered something Mimi had told her about good writing. She figured it applied to mystery solving too. "We've got to figure out the who?, what?, when?, where?, why?, and how?, before we go calling the authorities."

Evan stared out the window and scratched his head. He wondered what Christina would do.

Papa interrupted their thoughts. "I've got a surprise. You two seem so interested in alligators I thought you might enjoy a quick visit to The Conservancy room. A guest speaker is there this morning."

Avery tucked the notepad back in her pocket and said, "Great idea, Papa! We need all the information about alligators we can get!" She didn't tell him why.

"What's a conservancy?" Evan asked.

"It's an organization that helps people learn about and take care of the environment," Papa said. "Mimi and I are members of the one here in Palmetto Bluff. We want to help take care of this special place. When Captain William Hilton came here in the 1600s, he thought he'd landed in paradise."

Evan admired the tall palmetto trees that gave the community its name. With their green fronds waving in the gentle breeze, they seemed to tickle the sky like a feather duster. "It still looks like paradise to me!" Evan said.

The Conservancy room was decorated with posters and more displays with mounted wildlife similar to the ones they'd seen at the

Savannah National Wildlife Refuge. Avery and Evan were surprised to see other kids their age. Apparently Papa wasn't the only grandparent with this idea. Evan was also surprised to see Ranger Karen. He hoped she wouldn't remember him as the kid who wore the gator skull on his head.

"She must be making breakfast for us!" Avery said when she saw that Ranger Karen was holding a basket of eggs.

Evan raised his hand and shouted, "I'll have mine over easy!"

"I don't think you'd want to eat these eggs," Ranger Karen said. "For one thing, they might bite you on the way down."

When the ranger held up one of the eggs, Evan could see that it was white and a little bit larger than a chicken egg.

"This is an alligator egg," she explained. "Every spring, the mama alligators build a nest out of mud and plants that's about three feet tall. They lay anywhere from 30 to 50 eggs in the nest and cover them with more mud and plants. The eggs hatch in August and September."

"They must be hatching now!" Evan whispered to Avery.

"How do they get out?" a kid in the far corner asked.

"The baby alligators have a special egg tooth on the end of their snouts," she said. "When they're ready to hatch they make a chirping sound. The mother alligator digs open the nest and the babies break open their shells with the tooth."

Avery was still thinking about the numbers. "They have a lot of kids to take care of," she said.

"Alligators don't really care for their young the way humans do," Ranger Karen said. "But the mother does guard her nest from **predators** such as raccoons that like to eat the eggs. After they hatch, she continues to watch over them until they're large enough to protect themselves."

Ranger Karen's expression grew very serious. "That's why it's very important to stay away from alligators. Humans are not their prey, but they will attack if they think their young are being threatened."

Evan punched Avery with his elbow and giggled. "I'll stick with chicken eggs from the grocery store," he said.

Ranger Karen held up a picture of a baby alligator. Avery was surprised that it had yellowish stripes across its body.

"These stripes help camouflage the babies to blend in with the marsh while they hunt their own food," she said. "They eat insects, worms, and other small prey. And sadly, sometimes the baby gators become food for other animals. It's all a part of the food chain that keeps nature in balance."

Avery's mind was racing. A shiver ran up her spine. *She hoped that she and Evan wouldn't become part of the food chain before they got to the bottom of their mystery!*

Watch out for baby gators! Mimi
and Papa had to stop The Ladybug
golf cart to wait for this little
gator to cross the road!

11

MIRACULOUS MUNCHERS

After the lecture, Avery and Evan got to hold one of the alligator eggs. Evan was afraid a baby alligator might come out and bite him with its egg tooth. "Don't worry," Ranger Karen reassured him. "This egg has been preserved. It will never hatch."

"I would love to see a real baby alligator," Avery said. The big ones still grossed her out, but she thought a baby one might be cute—like a puppy or a kitten.

"I wish I had one to show you," Ranger Karen said. "Sadly, we haven't seen a lot of **hatchlings** this year. It's very strange. In fact, there are several scientists doing studies right now to find out what has happened in the environment to cause the problem. We're going to assign numbers to the ones we can find, so we can keep track of them."

Evan whispered in Avery's ear. "Maybe it's because the poachers have nabbed all the mama gators!"

That comment made Avery think of the post office note. "How would someone go about getting an alligator tooth?" she asked. She hoped the ranger would think she was curious and not suspect she was investigating a mystery.

"Well, of course you could kill an alligator and pull its teeth out," she said. "But without a permit, you'd go to jail. You also might be lucky enough to find one. Scientists believe that an alligator can re-grow each of its teeth about fifty times."

Evan stuck his tongue in the gap where he'd lost a front tooth during the summer. "I wish I was so lucky," he said.

"How many teeth do alligators have?" Avery asked.

"About eighty," the ranger said.

Evan was making marks in the air with his fingers. Avery, who knew he was doing mental math, handed him her smart phone. "Use the calculator," she said.

"Unbelievable!" Evan said. "One alligator could grow 4,000 teeth during its life!"

Now, Avery was more confused than ever. Maybe the camo guy in the post office found that tooth he was wearing.

Papa thanked the ranger for coming and asked if she knew where the fish were biting. "I hear they've been reeling them in from the May River in Bluffton," she said.

"You tadpoles ready to go and catch some fish?" Papa asked.

Avery and Evan exchanged excited glances. Papa thought it was because they were eager to catch fish. Avery and Evan knew it was because Bluffton was exactly where they wanted to go next. That's where the notepad had come from and they hoped to find more clues there.

During the short drive to Bluffton, Papa told them that he'd read in the local paper about some alligator sightings on the May

River. "We need to keep our eyes peeled," he said.

"I wish we had Clue along," Evan said. "He loves the water and he could protect us from gators."

"Oh, no!" Papa said. "Dogs are just the right size for alligators. We wouldn't want Clue to become a tasty snack!"

"We'll have to take him along next time we go to the beach," Avery said. "No worries about gators there."

"Don't be so sure," Papa said. "Alligators do usually live in fresh water, but recently one came walking out of the ocean at Hilton Head. Those sunbathers may never go in the water again!"

If someone was nabbing gators, Avery thought, why were there so many sightings?

The main street in the little town's historic center, known as Old Bluffton, was lined with interesting shops. Windows displayed antiques and quirky folk art, and whirligigs of every sort spun crazily in the autumn breeze.

Papa pulled into a **decrepit** little bait shop on the edge of town, "to find out what they're biting," he said. Avery suspected Papa was more interested in buying soda and boiled peanuts. Avery thought the place looked like it belonged in the middle of a swamp. The inside smelled damp and musty, sort of like the mushrooms in Mimi's refrigerator. The rough board floors had splintery cracks and groaned under their footsteps.

A thin man, who looked as ancient as the local oak trees, got up from a creaky wood chair to help them. Grey stubble hid in his wrinkles and popped out as he talked. "What kin I help ya with?" he drawled. "If ya need bait, I'd go with them crickets. Catfish is crazy 'bout 'em."

Avery and Evan poked their noses against the wire cage and watched the man catch enough crickets to fill a small box. When he leaned over, they saw a large alligator tooth dangling from his neck. When the old man saw the kids staring at it, he proudly waved it at them.

"Somethin', ain't it?" he said. "Years ago, I used to catch gators with my brother—he lives out on Alligator Alley."

Avery and Evan immediately thought about Mr. Creepy they'd seen pulling the boat. *Was this his brother?*

The old man continued. "Anytime somebody had a gator come 'round their house, they'd call us and we'd haul 'em to the swamp and let 'em go."

"If you let them go," Avery said, "where'd you get that tooth?"

"Traded for it this morning," he said. "Young fella was buyin' some supplies and didn't have enough money."

"What kind of supplies?" Avery asked.

"Oh, just odds and ends you'd need for huntin', and some duct tape," he answered.

Avery knew that duct tape was strong enough to use for a lot of things. *Was it strong enough to hold gator jaws shut?*

12

GOBBLED GATOR

The May River ambled by the town as slow as the old man's speech. The gently moving water was **pristine** and almost as smooth as a pond. Avery imagined it looked much the same as when the early English explorers saw it for the first time and fished from its banks.

Evan and Avery carried the fishing gear while Papa carried a red polka-dot folding chair. Avery giggled at the sight. She knew he'd grabbed Mimi's chair by mistake.

Papa settled into his chair, stuck a wriggling cricket with his hook and jammed his fishing pole into the mushy mud. Soon, he was snoring softly.

"I guess he's exhausted from taking care of Mimi," Avery said.

Evan threw his first cricket out into the gentle current. He quickly felt a tug, but when he yanked his pole, all he'd caught was his own half-eaten cricket.

Avery honestly didn't feel like fishing. She was too fidgety trying to wrap her head around the mystery of all that had happened. Evan stuck his tongue out the side of his mouth as he carefully chose his next cricket victim. That was a sure sign that he was determined.

"I'm going for a little walk," Avery said. She was glad she was wearing her purple shoes since they were quickly becoming caked with thick mud, something she would have hated to see on her favorite turquoise sneakers. Evan had pulled off his shoes right away and rolled his pants up to his knees.

A white heron down the bank watched Avery suspiciously. He craned his neck out like he was clearing his throat to make a speech.

The **cicadas** sang like thousands of rattlesnakes all shaking their rattles at the same time. When one stopped singing, there were always hundreds more to pick up the tune. Occasionally, a chirping frog would join the chorus.

Avery stopped to admire a butterfly that was perched by the water's edge, slowly raising and lowering its wings while it drank water from the wet soil. She thought about how appropriate the insect's name was. Its color reminded her of the butter Mimi would always lay out on the counter to soften. While she was looking at the ground, she saw something she recognized.

"Evan, come here!" she yelled. She poked at something white, half buried in the mud.

"That looks like an alligator eggshell!" Evan said. He dug it out for a closer look. The leathery piece of shell looked like it had hatched weeks before. "There must have been a—"

Avery held up her hand. She heard a sound that was not a cicada or a frog. It was a cross between a bird and a whimpering puppy. "Evan, I think we'd better get out of here," she said.

Before they could run back to Papa, the heron hopped toward them. It was flapping wild wings as it thrust its long beak into the tall grass like a spear.

"It's caught a lizard!" Evan said.

Avery looked through the binoculars as the bird flew to a nearby rock. "I don't think that's a lizard," she said. "That's a baby alligator!"

The kids watched in horror as the heron gulped the little gator down. They could still see its outline as it wiggled in the bird's neck. "How awful!" Avery cried.

"That's what happens in the good ol' food chain!" Evan said as he ran back to Papa with Avery close on his heels. "I wonder where the mama is!"

Avery didn't know the answer for sure. But as she was watching the heron, she saw a man pulling a camouflage boat out of the river. *He looked an awful lot like Mr. Creepy.*

13

DEADLY CAMOUFLAGE?

The kids woke Papa and told him their frightening story. "Sorry I slept through all the excitement," he said.

Papa pulled up his fishing line to find a frisky catfish on the hook.

"I can't believe it," Evan said. "You can catch fish with your eyes closed."

"Let's release him," Papa said. "You can catch him next time."

An hour later, when Evan still hadn't caught a fish, Papa suggested that a fish on the plate was better than two in the river.

Avery watched Evan walk far enough into the water to wash the mud off his feet.

She noticed that he was limping. "What's wrong with your foot?" she asked.

Evan picked up his left foot and propped it on his knee. "I must have stepped on something when we were running."

"Let me see that," Avery said. She was surprised that Evan's foot was covered in tiny red squares. It made Avery think of the arrays she'd had to make in math class. In the center she could see the faint imprint of a letter "M." She quickly snapped a picture with her phone.

At Captain Woody's restaurant, they waited eagerly for their food while listening to someone play a guitar in the corner. None of them realized how hungry they'd gotten. Evan and Papa got catfish and hushpuppies. Papa also ordered a plate of raw oysters, which he slurped right out of the shell. Evan wouldn't touch them. "Too much like boogers," he said.

Avery, who was still grossed out by the sight of the poor gobbled gator, decided on turf instead of surf. She had just finished her last bite of hamburger when two motorcycles roared by. Both men were wearing camouflage, except for their helmets, which were sparkly blue. She heard the bikes screech to a stop just down the road.

"Wearing camo on a motorcycle seems dumb," Avery said. "How can you sneak up on something on a noisy motorcycle?"

"Yeah," Evan agreed. "I don't get it. If they're camouflaged, why do I still see them?"

"It's very scientific," Papa said. "You can see them because they're not hiding in the woods. Camouflage is designed specifically for the environment where it's going to be used."

That made Avery wonder if someone wearing camouflage had been watching them and they didn't even know. It was a scary thought.

"Remember that gator in the lagoon?" Papa said. "We almost couldn't see him because he was camouflaged. Even his **scales** and scutes helped him blend into his environment."

When he went to pay for the meal, Papa ran into an old friend. While they chatted, Christina and Evan walked down the street. They hadn't gone far when they noticed the motorcycles parked in a small alley. The blue helmets were resting on the seats, and Avery noticed that a lot of mud was splattered on the black fenders. She peeked into one of the saddlebags to see three rolls of duct tape. One of these camo dudes was their friend from the post office, all right!

"Let's see if we can find them," Avery whispered. They snuck down the alley, hugging the wall as they made their way. They quickly found themselves beneath an outdoor balcony. Three men clomped around above them.

"It has to happen tomorrow," a grave, raspy voice said. "You have to get them out of the way, or you'll never get what you need. If you're not careful, this could be deadly!"

14

JARRING DISCOVERY

"Get back, you scurvy scalawags!" Evan stabbed the air with an imaginary sword as they climbed flights of curved steps at the Palmetto Bluff Treehouse. It was a favorite hangout for area kids and luckily a short bike ride from Mimi and Papa's house. Avery couldn't even imagine the engineering skill it took to design the four-story treehouse around the massive oak tree.

"Haven't you forgotten your lizard pirate earring?" Avery teased. "Want me to catch you another one?"

"No thanks!" Evan said as he jabbed another make-believe villain and dashed to the top floor of the treehouse. He liked to pretend it was the crow's nest of a pirate ship.

Avery climbed out onto one of the giant oak tree's limbs that grew right through a third floor window. She stretched out like a gator basking in the sun to warm its cold-blooded body and soaked in the autumn warmth. When she rubbed her hand across the rough, scaly tree bark, she wondered, *Is this what it feels like to pet an alligator?* Avery really hoped she'd never find out.

Closing her eyes, Avery let her mind replay the conversation they'd heard in Bluffton the day before. Hadn't Christina warned her that mysteries could get them into big trouble? Avery didn't know that big trouble could mean deadly trouble. She wondered what Christina would do in her situation. She thought of calling her on the phone, but that would only be admitting that she had gotten in over her head in her very first mystery. Besides, Christina was a responsible adult now. She would probably put a stop to any flirtation with danger.

"Let's go see if that guy's catching any tadpoles!" Evan yelled down to Avery.

"What guy?" Avery asked, cracking one eye open to see what her brother was up to. Now his fists were curled in front of one eye like an imaginary telescope as he pretended to survey the area.

Avery slid off her perch and jogged up another flight of stairs to join Evan at the top floor railing. As she looked over the treetops, she was thankful for the heavy ropes between the floor and railing that were tied in the shape of diamonds to keep them from falling. Every time she saw that shape, she remembered that her teacher taught them that the diamond shape is also called a rhombus, a member of the quadrilateral family.

A young man with dark hair squatted by the water's edge in the distance. "That guy looks a little old to be catching tadpoles," Avery said. "Let's find out what he's up to."

"Hey!" the young man greeted them as they approached. Avery could see that he was scooping water into jars.

"What are you catching?" Evan asked.

"Water," the young man said. "I have to send it off to be tested for pollution."

"Are you a scientist?" Avery asked, remembering that Ranger Karen told them that scientists were trying to figure out why there weren't many baby alligators this year.

"No," the young man replied. "I'm just a scientist's assistant. I got a summer job at the refuge to earn money for college. It's very expensive, you know. I want to be an engineer."

"What kind of engineer?" Avery asked.

"I'm not sure yet," the young man answered. "I just like to design things. You know, 'a better way to build a mousetrap' kind of stuff."

"You said you got a job at the refuge, but this isn't on the refuge," Avery said.

"Well, this same water runs through the refuge," he said. 'I'm collecting samples all over the area."

"Better check this over here," Evan suggested. He picked up a rock and threw it in a small puddle. "This water looks brown and yucky. It must be polluted."

"Not necessarily," the young man replied. "That was probably caused by tannin."

"You mean the water got sunburned?" Evan asked.

The young man's laughter echoed across the water. "Tannin is a chemical compound found in rotting wood and leaves. Leaves probably fell into that water. The tannin leached into the water and turned it dark."

"Hmm, interesting," Evan said. "I'll have to check that out on my iPad. And, in case you want to know, I hate leeches."

Before the young man could explain the difference between leach and leech, his cell phone rang and he answered it. "You're kidding!" he said, as his expression turned serious. "I told you to be careful. Yeah, give me the address."

The young man scribbled something on a piece of paper and said, "Sorry, kids. Gotta go." When he threw on his backpack, Avery could hear jangling metal. She wondered why someone gathering water samples in jars would be carrying metal.

After the young man had run past the treehouse and disappeared from sight, Evan noticed he'd left something behind. It was a jar of water.

"Evan," Avery exclaimed. "Does that jar look familiar to you?"

"Seen one jar, seen 'em all," Evan said.

"No," she said. "Look carefully! That's the same kind of jar the firefly note was in!"

Avery had a sneaking suspicion that this young man was interested in something besides water.

The Palmetto Bluff Treehouse is
nestled in a huge oak tree!

15

FOOT IN MOUTH

Back at the treehouse, Avery was climbing on her bike when she noticed a scrap of paper on the ground. "Evan, I think the water guy dropped this," she said. "It's the address of a doctor's office."

Avery slapped her hand with the note. "I'm not feeling very well," she said. "I have a terrible stomachache."

Evan looked concerned. "Did you eat Mimi's bread?" he asked.

Avery gave Evan a sly wink, "Yeah, something like that. I need to go and see..." She looked at the note again, "Dr. Grady."

"Ohhhhh!" Evan said. "I get it."

Papa drove Avery to the doctor's office and Evan went along, "for moral support," he'd said.

"I've made so many trips to the doctor's office since your Mimi broke her leg, I should be a Ph.D. by now," Papa complained.

At the doctor's office, Papa signed Avery in and explained that he needed to run an errand. "I should be back before you see the doctor," he said.

Avery and Evan scouted the waiting room. There was no sign of the water guy.

"Maybe he hasn't gotten here yet," Avery whispered as she chose a seat that would allow her to see the entire waiting room.

Evan shuffled through a stack of old magazines, and not finding anything that interested him, picked up the local newspaper. "Look at this!" he said, showing the paper to Avery. A headline above the fold exclaimed: Baby Alligator Population Diminishing, Scientists Search for Answer. "What does diminishing mean?" Evan asked.

"It means there are fewer of them," Avery said.

Suddenly, a nurse opened the door to the waiting room. Avery tensed, thinking she was coming for her. Instead, a young man on crutches hobbled through the door. He was dressed in camouflage and the white bandage on his foot was soaked with blood. Evan and Avery were surprised to see a face they recognized. The water guy was helping his injured friend!

"You're lucky you still have a foot," the nurse said. "You can expect some bleeding. We'll need to check those stitches in a couple of days."

Avery and Evan held the newspaper in front of their faces and listened as the two men walked by. "Great going, Bozo," the water guy said. "Now we're short-handed at the refuge. If we miss our delivery tonight, I may bite your other foot!"

As soon as they were gone, Avery exhaled. She hadn't even realized she'd been holding her breath. "Evan, I think something with razor-sharp teeth almost had a foot for lunch," she said.

"Yeah," Evan agreed. "Or a peanut butter and toe jam sandwich."

The nurse burst back into the waiting room holding the water guy's backpack. "That man forgot this," she said.

Avery thought fast. "We'll take the backpack to him," she volunteered. "We know where he works."

"Thank you!" she said, handing Avery the jangling backpack.

Avery couldn't believe her luck! She didn't need her stomachache anymore. She pulled out her phone and punched 2. That was Papa's number on speed dial.

"It's a miracle!" she told Papa. "Can you pick us up?"

Avery didn't feel like she was fibbing. It truly was a miracle that they now had the excuse they needed to get back to the refuge! *She had a good idea that the "delivery" the men were talking about had something to do with alligators, and she intended to stop it!*

16

A BETTER MOUSETRAP?

"Papa, can we please spend the afternoon at the refuge?" Avery begged. She had already explained her promise to return the backpack and he'd agreed to drive them there before they went home.

"I would love to spend an afternoon at the refuge," he said. "But, believe it or not, I have to take someone else to the doctor. Mimi has an appointment."

"We'd be fine there," Avery continued. "If we need you, I've got my phone."

"I'll make a deal with you," Papa said. "If Ranger Karen is there, I'll let you stay."

Avery crossed her fingers.

"Aren't you gonna look inside?" Evan whispered, pointing at the backpack.

Avery nodded. She gingerly unfastened the buckle and lifted the flap. She wasn't surprised to find a small jar of water wrapped in bubble wrap. But the other items did surprise her!

"Evan, does this look familiar?" she whispered as she pulled out a piece of wire mesh about one foot square. In the center was an "M."

Evan looked puzzled.

Avery pulled out her smart phone and showed Evan the picture she'd made of the bottom of his foot during their fishing trip.

"That's the piece of wire I stepped on?" he asked.

"Probably not the same one, but one just like it," she said. "And look at this—a receipt from that bait shop in Bluffton. It's for something called Mason wire—I guess that's what the "M" stands for—and screws, springs and latches."

"Couldn't you use those things to make a mousetrap?" Evan asked. "He said something about a mousetrap."

"I think he's engineered a trap all right, but I'll bet it has nothing to do with mice," Avery said.

17

ZIG OR ZAG?

At the refuge, Avery's lucky streak continued. Ranger Karen was there and promised Papa she'd be there all afternoon. "They'll be fine as long as they stick to the main road near the center," she told him. "And don't bother any wildlife!" she reminded the kids.

"I'll be back as soon as Mimi sees the doctor!" Papa said, giving each of them one of his bear hugs. "You two scamps stay out of trouble!"

Avery smiled sweetly and wondered how many different names Papa had for them. "Scamps" was a new one she'd have to look up. She figured it was another of his synonyms for mischief-maker.

After leaving the backpack in the visitors' center as promised, they walked outside. Avery quickly noticed there were two motorcycles parked in the parking lot. There was also a very familiar old truck with its scaly paint and white door. There was a boat trailer behind it, but no boat. Just to make sure, Avery flipped back to the picture she'd made of the tag on Alligator Alley. It was definitely Mr. Creepy's rig.

"They're here!" she said. But Avery knew finding the men on the 29,000-acre refuge would be as difficult as finding a toothless alligator, especially since Mr. Creepy was obviously in a boat. The easiest thing to do, she thought, is to sit in this parking lot and wait until they returned. But what would that prove? She needed solid evidence that these men were taking alligators. She wanted to do everything possible to stop their delivery!

"Let's go!" Avery told Evan. "We don't have much time."

But something else had already snagged Evan's attention. "Did you know this place was a rice plantation before the Civil War?" Evan asked as he stopped to read a historical marker. "It became a national wildlife refuge in 1927."

Any other time, Avery would have loved knowing that. She loved history. But now, she was on a mission. "I think I liked you better before you learned to read," she snapped. "We don't have time to read markers!"

Evan noticed that Avery was becoming quite bossy! Girls!

They walked along a dirt road, stepping to the side each time an occasional car poked past them like a Sunday driver and left them in a cloud of sandy, white dust. Evan was getting impatient.

"We've been walking a long time and haven't seen anything but rubberneckers," he said, referring to the people craning their necks out of car windows hoping to see wildlife without leaving the safety and comfort of their cars.

"Who knows what could be around this curve?" Avery said, pointing to the bend in the road ahead. But as soon as they rounded it, she was as disappointed as Evan. There was nothing interesting.

Avery checked the time on her phone. Time was running out.

"Let's go this way," Evan suggested. He had spotted a narrow cobblestone path that slithered into the woods like a curious snake.

Despite her better judgment, Avery agreed. The path led them under trees so heavy with moss that they almost blocked out the sun. "I feel like I'm walking through a hairy cave," Evan said.

When the kids heard something rustling in the fallen leaves beside the path, they froze. "Think that could be a gator?" Avery asked. She was already wondering if they'd made a mistake walking here alone.

"Aren't you supposed to run away from a gator in a z-z-zig-z-z-zag pattern?" Evan asked through chattering teeth. He moved his feet from side to side as if warming up.

"I don't think that's true," Avery said, trying not to panic. "I read you should run straight away from them as fast as you possibly can. Alligators can run about 10 miles per hour. Adult humans can run about 15 miles per hour."

"So, we can outrun them by five miles per hour!" Evan said.

"I said adults, Evan!" Avery replied. "We're not adults! We just have to be very careful not to get close enough for a gator to chase us. We wouldn't want it to be a tie!"

The rustling sound stopped abruptly. Avery had already grabbed Evan's hand to run when a chubby beaver waddled onto the path. He stood on his hind legs and stared at them as if he were waiting to be served afternoon tea. Then he slapped his thick tail on the ground and waddled away.

Evan giggled nervously. "It's almost like he was trying to tell us something," Evan said.

"Maybe he was," Avery said as she walked to where the beaver had disappeared into the woods. "Look at this!"

It was a piece of camouflage fabric. Its ripped edge was tinged with dried blood.

"We must be on the right track," Avery said. If it had been a risk to leave the road, Avery knew it was an even bigger risk to leave the cobblestone path. She quickly checked her phone. The little battery symbol was half full.

Their shoes kicked up a colorful confetti of freshly fallen leaves as they trudged through the woods. Soon, the land sloped downward so steeply that they had to lean back to keep their balance.

"Hang on a second," Evan said. "I need to tie my shoe."

"Better not lean..." Avery was going to say forward, but before she could get the word out, Evan was rolling head over heels down the hill like a roly-poly with blonde hair.

Avery chased after him as his screams of, "HELLLLLPPP!" struggled to keep up with him. But before she could catch him Evan plowed into a pine tree with a thud. The tree shivered and sprinkled him with reddish-brown pine needles.

"Are you OK?" Avery asked, fearing that Mimi might not be the only one with a broken leg now.

Evan picked a pine needle out of his hair. "Yeah, thanks to this nice tree," he said. In response, the tree released a pinecone the size of a grenade that plunked Evan on the head.

Avery laughed with relief. "I think you should say thanks to this naughty tree," she said.

Evan looked up to make sure another pinecone wasn't headed his way. That was when he saw it—a note was flapping against the trunk. It was held there with duct tape.

Before Avery could read the note, they heard something running through the leaves, but saw nothing. Was it another animal? Or was it someone wearing camouflage that blended with the woods?

She pulled the note from the pine tree and read:

Please stay away!
Kids are no match for
alligators!

18

SLIPPERY SLIDE

Retreat back up the hill...or keep going? After all, the note was true. They were no match for alligators. Avery thought of Christina again. Not the new, college student Christina, but the old, mystery-solving Christina. What would she do? Avery knew the answer. They had to keep going. Avery smiled and tried not to let Evan see how scared she was.

Soon the ground became level again, but the brush grew thick. They pushed their way through a stand of cattails.

"They look like corn dogs stuck on spears," Evan said. "A corn dog sure would be good right about now! It's waaaay past snack time. I'm so hungry I think I could eat Mimi's bread!"

Some of the cattails had burst open to reveal fluffy seed heads. It reminded Avery of teddy bear stuffing as it drifted in the wind like snow. She knew that cattails always grew close to water. She also knew that snakes and alligators did too.

"Watch where you're walking, Evan," she warned.

Finally, they found themselves standing on a narrow finger of land jutting out into the water. "Let's sit here and rest for a minute," Evan said, wiping the sweat off his forehead.

Avery was thirsty. She wished she had brought a water bottle. Although there was water all around them, she knew they shouldn't drink it. It was filled bacteria and organisms that could make them sick.

"Ouch!" Avery held her forearm even with her eyes and watched a mosquito's **abdomen** fill with her blood. She slapped it into an ugly red smear. "That'll teach you, Mister Mosquito," she said.

"That wasn't Mister Mosquito," Evan said. "That was Mrs. Mosquito."

"Did you know her personally?" Avery asked with a hint of sarcasm.

"No," Evan said. "But I do know that only female mosquitoes bite. The males feed on flower nectar."

"Been Googling mosquitoes, huh?" Avery said, already knowing the answer. "Well, maybe it thought I was a beautiful flower."

Evan rolled his eyes. "Sure," he said. "A case of mistaken identity, just like with the alligators and crocodiles."

Avery was surprised at how quiet things were. She was glad they hadn't encountered any alligators, but wasn't this a perfect habitat for them?

Evan got up and walked farther out onto the little finger of land. It was fringed with thick grass and weeds, but Evan saw something that captured his interest. "We've been sitting here sweating," he said, "and this is a swimming hole! See, the rangers have even built a slide into the water!"

Dividing the grass like the part in a fresh haircut was a wide, slick area of mud that slipped into the water. "I'm going in!"

Evan announced as he pulled off his shoes and plopped his bottom onto the slide.

Before Avery could stop him, Evan was slipping into the water. "Wheeeeeeeee!" he shouted, anticipating the cool splash ahead. But his feet hit something much harder than water. His joyful cry turned to shouts of terror.

"Help!" he screamed. "A gator's got me! HELLLLPPPP!"

19

DANGEROUSLY CUTE

Avery knew that Evan was often **melodramatic**, but this time, she didn't think he was over-reacting. Thankful for the strong muscles she'd developed as a cheerleader, she tugged at Evan's outstretched arms with all her might. Several tugs later, Evan's foot finally popped free.

She looked down the slide, fully expecting to see an alligator's gaping gullet, but instead she saw a bit of metal glinting in the late afternoon sun.

"There's no alligator," she reassured Evan, who was heaving on the ground like a fish out of water. "But I think I know what it is. Be quiet and listen."

In a few minutes, they could hear mournful chirps. Avery recognized them from their fishing trip on the May River.

She crawled to the slide and asked Evan to hold onto her ankles as she reached down to the bottom. "Pull!" she ordered.

When Evan got her back to the top of the slide, she was dragging what looked like a muddy box covered with weeds. "This is it!" she said, clearing away the debris to reveal a metal box trap with wire mesh sides identical to the wire they'd seen in the book bag. Peering from inside were two baby alligators!

Evan wiggled the handle on top. "That must be what my foot got caught in," he said.

"I knew our water boy wasn't interested in catching mice!" Avery said. "He has engineered a special trap for catching baby alligators!"

"So that's why there haven't been many baby alligators this year!" Evan said.

"Exactly!" Avery exclaimed.

"You know, they're kinda cute," Evan said, placing his hands on the trap to admire the little, yellow-striped alligators.

"Watch out, Evan!" Avery warned. "They may be cute, but they still have very sharp teeth! Keep your hands away from them!"

"I wonder where their mother is," Evan said curiously.

"That is strange," Avery agreed, even though she was glad the mother was nowhere in sight. If she were nearby, Avery knew she would attack them to protect her babies. Besides, she felt sure the camo men had moved these babies far from their nest.

"I guess you should get in touch with Ranger Karen," Evan said.

"Right," Avery agreed, reaching for her phone. But before she could pull it out of her pocket, they heard the sound of a boat motor. Speeding toward them, it sounded a lot like Evan when he was making a raspberry with his mouth.

"We'd better hide," Avery said, motioning for Evan to follow her back into the cattails. The boat sputtered to a stop and its driver threw out an anchor. It landed right beside Evan's shoe!

Avery quietly parted the cattails and peeked through them. She recognized the camouflaged boat they had followed down Alligator Alley. Its driver looked out from under the brim of his camouflaged cap with beady eyes. Even though she'd only seen him in the rearview mirror of his truck, Avery knew it was Mr. Creepy!

"It's OK, little fellers," Mr. Creepy told the baby alligators as he stepped out of the boat and lifted the trap. "You'll like your new home! Now, let's see if we can find some more of your friends."

Avery knew this was their only chance to know for sure what was happening to the baby alligators. She placed her finger to her lips and motioned for Evan to stay low and follow her. Avery slipped through the cattails into the shallow water. Mr. Creepy's boat had drifted sideways and was parallel to the bank. The front half of it was covered with a large silvery tarp. Avery lifted a corner and crawled into the boat, helping Evan slip in behind her.

They held their breath as Mr. Creepy gently placed the baby gators in the boat and pushed them under the tarp. They felt the boat rock as he pushed it away from the bank and then jumped in.

They could hear soft, mournful chirping, but Avery knew it was coming from more than two baby alligators. She quietly pulled out her phone and turned on the flashlight app, being careful that its rays didn't shine out from under the tarp. Avery couldn't believe her eyes! At least 40 little red dots shined in its beam, before Avery turned off the app. She knew that alligator eyes shined red in the dark.

Waiting until Mr. Creepy started the noisy boat motor, Avery whispered to Evan, "I'll bet he has at least twenty baby gators on this boat!"

20

NABBING THE NABBERS

The boat's front end rose out of the water as the boat picked up speed, occasionally bouncing up and down and rattling the metal cages. Avery and Evan hung on for dear life to another large tarp that was rolled up beside them like a sleeping bag. Avery wondered if that could have been what had fallen out of the boat when they were following it on Alligator Alley. At the time, she had thought it might be a large gator, but now she realized that Mr. Creepy only seemed interested in the babies.

BUMP! The boat slapped the water. Evan lost his grip on the rolled tarp and crashed into Avery. The collision knocked Avery's phone out of her hand and it slid across the metal boat's bottom and whacked one of the gator traps. She couldn't lose that phone!

Avery felt around in the darkness, being careful not to let her fingers get too close to the gator traps. Finally, she felt the familiar shape of her phone and pulled it close to her. When the boat stopped, Avery knew she wanted someone there to meet them who could nab the nabber!

First, Avery pulled up her mapping app. She knew the Global Positioning System, or GPS, would tell her exactly where they were. She watched the little blue dot moving along to show their position on the map, relieved that it was working, but surprised to see that they were now outside of the refuge. Her fingers danced around the screen as she next pulled up the phone's browser so she could look up the number for the refuge. When she punched in the number, the phone rang and rang, but no one answered. She checked the time. No wonder! Avery realized the visitors' center had already closed.

Next, she tried Papa's number. She imagined him sitting impatiently in the parking lot, wondering where they were. There was no answer. Avery remembered how Papa fussed about what he called "these new-fangled phones" and often forgot to plug his into the charger. *Was his phone dead?* Next she tried Mimi and Papa's house. Still no answer.

"No one's answering!" Avery whispered to Evan.

"Did you try Christina?" he asked.

That's right! Avery thought. *Didn't Christina say she was "only a phone call away"?!*

She punched Christina's number. It went straight to voicemail: "This is Christina. Please leave a message."

"Christina, we need you at the refuge!" Avery whispered as loudly as she dared into the phone.

21

FORMULA FRET

Christina watched a shadow creeping across her test paper. She glanced out the classroom window at the sunset and realized that her time was running out. Her mind wandered as she struggled to figure out the last problem on her test. If only she could remember those geometry formulas! She counted the crusty old bricks surrounding the window in Alexander Hall. The building had once been a flour mill, and once again Christina felt fortunate that she was attending school in such a historic town. There were eight bricks across the top and 11 bricks down the side. Length times width, she thought, recalling the simple formula for figuring area. It would take 88 of those bricks to fill in that window. But the perimeter would be length plus width plus length plus width. So there are 38 bricks surrounding that window.

Oh, yeah! The simple formulas had helped her remember the more complicated ones she needed to finish the problem. Her pencil was moving furiously when she felt her phone buzz in her pocket. There's no way she was chancing pulling it out. If her professor saw that, he might think she was looking up the answers.

Christina finished her test, turned it in, and darted for the door. As she walked to her Jeep, she checked her phone and smiled. A missed call from Avery. She probably wants to see how I did on my test, Christina thought as she placed the phone to her ear. Her expression quickly changed to a frown when she heard the message.

She jumped in her Jeep and headed for the refuge, thankful it was only a few miles away. She drove across the Savannah River as quickly as possible over the beautiful, tall bridge that looked like a sailboat. But her mind was going faster than her Jeep.

What had those kids gotten themselves into? Or more than likely, what kind of trouble had Evan dragged Avery into? What were they doing back at the refuge? Where was Papa? What about the humongous alligators there? Christina was very worried.

22

THE ALLIGATOR OR THE EGG?

Avery and Evan peeked out from under the tarp as the boat slowed and finally bobbed to a stop. The sun was sinking below the trees, but a short distance away, Avery could make out a small lagoon with wide earthen walls. Silhouetted in the soft purple twilight were all the characters she expected to see. Camo dude was hobbling along on his crutches and the water boy was shouting orders to several other men dressed in camo.

The men were dumping baby alligators from traps into wooden crates and nailing down the tops. The crates were then being stacked on a trailer hooked to a four-wheeler.

Avery and Evan heard Mr. Creepy muttering to himself, "Guess I'm too late to save any more," he said. "First the eggs and now the babies."

"What's he talking about?" Evan whispered.

Avery slowly shook her head. "I think we've had it all wrong," she said.

Avery watched as the water boy spotted Mr. Creepy. "Get out of here, old man!" he shouted across the water. "Didn't we warn you to stay away from our spots? If you don't leave, we might introduce you to a lagoon full of very hungry alligators!"

Avery was no longer afraid of Mr. Creepy. "Evan, she whispered, "I think Mr. Creepy has been trying to save the alligators!"

"They've been trapping the baby alligators!" Evan said. He pointed at camo dude and water boy.

"Yes, and stealing the eggs from the nests!" said Christina.

Before Mr. Creepy could respond, a sound like giant mosquitoes suddenly buzzed all around them. Three airboats, with their giant fans whirring, surrounded Mr. Creepy's boat and surveyed the lagoon with powerful spotlights. Avery could see there were uniformed rangers on two of the boats with bright searchlights. On the third were Papa and Christina with Ranger Karen.

One ranger hopped across to Mr. Creepy's boat and slapped handcuffs on him. The others rounded up the men at the lagoon.

Avery and Evan threw back the tarp. "We're here!" Avery called, waving her arms above her head.

"Thank goodness we were able to track your phone!" Christina exclaimed.

Papa helped them onto the airboat and the questions started flying. "Did these men kidnap you?" Ranger Karen asked.

"Why weren't you at the visitors' center?" demanded Papa.

"I can explain everything," Avery said. "But first I'd like to look inside that lagoon."

Ranger Karen pulled closer to the lagoon and aimed her spotlight at the water. It was filled with a seething mass of alligators. Others, their mouths and legs still taped with duct tape, were stacked along the sides like cordwood.

"I can't wait to hear your explanation!" Ranger Karen said to the red-faced camo dude and the slack-mouthed water boy.

23

GATOR RESCUERS

Back at the refuge visitors' center, Avery asked Ranger Karen to take the handcuffs off Mr. Creepy, who had said his name was Wilbur Bailey. "You can't take him to jail!" Avery said.

"But he's a poacher!" Ranger Karen said. "We caught him red-handed delivering two baby alligators to his cohorts at the lagoon."

"He was trying to rescue the baby alligators," Avery insisted.

"But what about those adult alligators penned up in the lagoon?" Papa asked.

"Maybe Mr. Bailey can explain that better than I can," Avery said. "But my theory is that they rounded up the adults to get them out of the way so they could raid the nests for eggs and hatchlings."

Mr. Bailey finally spoke. "That's exactly what they were doin'!" he said. "As soon as the females had laid their eggs, they'd catch 'em and take 'em to the lagoon along with any other gators near them. Then they could steal the eggs. Then they started trappin' the babies that came from any eggs they missed."

"But why didn't they just kill the adult alligators to get them out of the way?" Christina asked.

"If they did, there wouldn't be any babies the next year," Ranger Karen said. "It was smart to round up the adults since alligators are cannibals. A lot of baby alligators are eaten by other alligators. Very few hatchlings live to become adults."

Evan remembered the baby alligator the bird had gobbled. "I know!" he said.

"I hated to see it happening," Mr. Bailey said. "Once I saw what they were up to, I tried to watch where they put the traps and get the babies before they came back for 'em. I probably got more 'en a hundred at my place."

"On Alligator Alley?" Evan said.

"That's right," Mr. Bailey said. "Most folks don't want gators around. But I can't imagin' the Lowcountry without 'em. I was plannin' on turnin' all the babies loose once them bad fellers had cleared out."

"But what were those men doing with the eggs and babies?" Christina asked.

"There's a huge black market for wild alligators here and in foreign countries," Avery said, then whispered to Evan, "I borrowed your iPad."

"Yes," Ranger Karen agreed. "And it's a lot easier to ship eggs and babies than it is to ship adults! Those men were probably shipping them to someone up north who already had buyers all over the world."

"That's probably who he sent the note to when we saw him standing in the post office," Evan said.

"And the poachers were leaving notes for Mr. Bailey because they thought he was a poacher too!" Avery said.

"Yep," Mr. Bailey said. "I left a note myself when I saw you kids in the woods today.

I wanted to scare you away from the danger... but it didn't work." He frowned.

"Well, you should never have put yourselves in danger," Ranger Karen scolded the kids as she removed Mr. Bailey's handcuffs. "But thanks to you, those baby gators will likely live thirty-five to fifty years on the refuge. I only hope that if you're really interested in helping the alligators, you'll become biologists when you grow up."

Papa added his own scolding. "First Christina, and now you!" he said. "Why are my grandkids always sticking their noses into mysteries? And this time you could have gotten those noses bitten clean off!"

And then he, and the kids, thought of something really, really scary: MIMI!

"She will croak when she hears what we've been up to," Evan said, and shivered.

24

BREAD BAIT

Papa covered the picnic table with newspaper and poured the Lowcountry boil onto the table. "Everybody dig in!" he said.

Spread across the newspaper were little potatoes, corn on the cob, fat sausages, and best of all, shrimp, right out of the Atlantic Ocean, fresh-caught that very day.

"This is awesome," Evan said, turning his head sideways to read an interesting article beside a particularly large potato. "They've discovered a new kind of shark off the coast of South Carolina! Now that we know how to handle wild animals with deadly teeth, I wonder if they need any help with those!" He stabbed the potato and chomped it in half like an alligator.

Papa had invited Mr. Bailey and his bait shop brother named Jeb to dinner. When Mimi told Evan she'd found time to bake him more bread, he turned to Jeb. "Wouldn't you like some bread?" Evan asked. "*Lots* of it?"

Jeb looked sympathetic. "Let me show you something," he said. "Grab your fishing pole and a loaf of that, uh, bread."

The two disappeared, but thirty minutes later, Evan had a string of six fat catfish. He was grinning ear to ear. "That bread is better than worms," he whispered to Avery. "The catfish love it!"

"Hey, Mimi," Evan said. "Can you bake me a loaf to take home with me? And promise that you won't brush up on your math or science. Your bread is perfect just the way it is!"

Mimi gave him a puzzled luck as Christina passed out marshmallows for making S'mores over the backyard fire pit.

"I'm releasin' them baby alligators in a few days," Mr. Bailey said. "Would you kids like to watch?"

Avery and Evan eagerly looked at Mimi and Papa for permission.

"That's fine," Mimi said, "as long as you don't release them anywhere near here. If I break another leg, there's no way I can bake bread for Evan, and I think I will make some for his mom, and teachers, and friends—who knew he loved my bread so much? What a great grandson!"

Evan groaned loudly. Avery just laughed and laughed, until Mimi said, "Oh, for you, too, Miss Avery!"

When Papa roared about as loudly as a bull gator, Mimi looked suspicious. Christina put an end to the whole thing by stuffing a big, fat, roasted marshmallow into her grandfather's mouth. She smiled to herself in satisfaction.

Another crop of baby alligators safe, Mimi thought to herself, and a new crop of mystery-solvers, too!

The End

DO YOU LIKE MYSTERIES?

You have the chance to solve them!
You can solve little mysteries,
like figuring out
how to do your homework and
why your dog always hides your shoes.

You can solve big mysteries, like how to
program a fun computer game,
protect an endangered animal,
find a new energy source,
INVENT A NEW WAY TO DO SOMETHING, **explore**
outer space, and more!

You may be surprised to find
that **science**, **technology**,
engineering, **math**, and even
HISTORY, literature, and
ART can help you solve all kinds of
"mysteries" you encounter.

So feed your curiosity, learn all you can, apply
your creativity, and **be a mystery-solver too!**

– Carole Marsh

More about the Science, Technology,
Engineering, & Math in this book

1 TON = 2000 POUNDS

To convert tons to pounds:	To convert pounds to tons:
multiply the number of tons by 2000	divide the number of pounds by 2000

WHAT IS A RHOMBUS?

A rhombus is an equilateral parallelogram.

What does that mean?

- *It is a flat (2-dimensional) shape.*
- *It has 4 sides.*

- *All the sides are the same length.*
- *The sides opposite each other are parallel.*

All squares are rhombuses, but not all rhombuses are squares!

DEW POINT

When the temperature outside drops below the *dew point*, some of the moisture in the air changes from gas to liquid. This moisture released from the air forms as water droplets on the ground called *dew*.

See dew point graph and more info online!

HOW TO CALCULATE THE PERIMETER OF A RECTANGLE

length + width + length + width

length = 5 cm
width = 2 cm

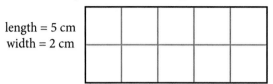

5 cm + 2 cm + 5 cm + 2 cm = 14 cm

HOW TO CALCULATE THE AREA OF A RECTANGLE

length x width

length = 5 cm
width = 2 cm

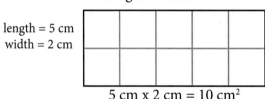

5 cm x 2 cm = 10 cm^2

ETYMOLOGY

The word *alligator* comes from the Spanish word *el lagarto*, meaning "the lizard."

URBAN DESIGN

The city of Savannah was designed by James Oglethorpe in the early 1700s. It was a unique and remarkable city plan! It had a repeated pattern of connected neighborhoods (called wards), each with its own central open space (called squares). Streets on the outside of each ward allow traffic to easily get from one area to the next, and streets on the inside of each ward lead to the square to make each neighborhood pedestrian-friendly.

The squares allow for more open space in Savannah than any city layout in history!

This diagram from 1770 shows one ward in Savannah. The small boxes are land where people could build houses. The large boxes are land for markets, schools, churches, and other public buildings. Oglethorpe Square is in the center.

See larger sketch online!

ALLIGATOR FACTS

- *Alligator Mississippiensis...*
  is the official name of the American Alligator!

- Alligators eat fish, turtles, mammals, birds, other reptiles...and, yes, even small dogs that get too close to gator-filled lagoons!

- An adult male alligator can grow as long as 15 feet, and can weigh close to 1,000 pounds! A female rarely grows larger than 9 feet long.

- The roar of a male alligator looking for a mate is, in a word—AWESOME!

- Female alligators dig a hole in a mound of mud and sticks and lay up to 50 eggs. Trust me, you NEVER want to get between a mom gator and her nest!

- Are baby alligators boys or girls? It depends! At a nest temperature of 93°F or more, most will be boys; at 86°F or below, girls. Babies are between 4½ and 8 inches long.

- Unless a wading bird, eagle, big fish, or sea turtle eats them for lunch, alligators grow ONE FOOT A YEAR until they reach maturity!

- Alligators are amazing creatures dating back to prehistoric times! They deserve our respect (and not just because they have powerful jaws filled with big teeth!).

- Never approach or harass an alligator!

DON'T FEED THE ALLIGATORS

- NEVER EVER feed an alligator! If you do, they will probably have to be killed because they will associate humans with food. "Can't we just relocate them?" you might ask. No. Alligators have the best homing instincts of any animal; they will travel up to 100 miles or more to get back to their home lagoon. "A fed alligator is a dead alligator."

APEX PREDATORS

- Once an alligator reaches six feet long, it is known as an "apex predator"...it has no other predators to worry about (except bigger gators!).

Here is a partial list of other apex predators:

On Land:
African Lion
American Badger
Boa Constrictor
Cheetah
Chimpanzee
Grizzly Bear
Human
King Cobra
Polar Bear
Tiger

In the Air:
Bald Eagle
Great Horned Owl
Harrier Hawk
Osprey

In Aquatic Environments:
Alligator Snapping Turtle
American Alligator
American Crocodile
Blue Whale
Bull Shark
Electric Eel
Giant Grouper
Giant Pacific Octopus
Giant Salamander
Great Barracuda
Great White Shark
Grey Whale
Humpback Whale
Marlin
Orca
Tiger Shark
Tuna

(GPS)
GLOBAL POSITIONING SYSTEM

The Global Positioning System (GPS) is a network of approximately 30 satellites orbiting the Earth.

Wherever you are on the planet, at least four GPS satellites are always 'visible.' Each one transmits information about its position and the current time at regular intervals. These signals travel at the speed of light.

Your GPS device (such as a cell phone) can receive the signals the satellites broadcast. Your GPS device calculates how far away each satellite is based on how long it took for the messages to arrive. Once your GPS device has information from at least three satellites, it can pinpoint your location using a process called **trilateration**.

Trilateration:

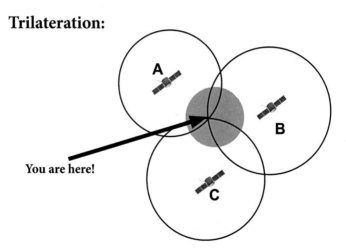

GLOSSARY

SAD **abdomen** – area below the chest, where stomach and other organs are located; belly

alligator – a large crocodilian reptile that has a thick, tough skin, a long body and tail, sharp teeth, and a short broad snout; found in tropical areas in the southeastern United States and China

archaeologist – a scientist who studies past human life and culture using information gained from the analysis of artifacts such as pottery, tools, and buildings

camouflaged – concealed by coloring or covering that imitates the surroundings

SAD **cantankerous** - ill-tempered; difficult to deal with

crocodile – any of various large reptiles with thick, tough skin, a long body and tail, sharp teeth, and a long pointed snout; found in tropical swamps

cicada – a large insect characterized by thin membranous wings and a shrill noise emitted by the male

SAD **decrepit** – broken or worn out from age or lack of care

ecosystem – a community of living things, together with their environments

SAD **exasperated** – excited with anger or frustration

SAD **extinction** – when something is no longer in existence because it has died out completely

food chain – a succession of living organisms in which each serves as food for the next

geometry – the mathematical study of objects such as points, lines, planes, and solid figures

habitat – the natural environment of a plant or animal

hatchling – a young bird, reptile, or fish recently emerged from an egg

humidity – the amount of water vapor in the air

iridescent – shining with different colors when seen from different angles

melodramatic – overly excited or sensational

paleontologist – a scientist who studies fossils to understand living things from former geologic periods

predator – an animal that kills and eats other animals

predicament – a difficult, trying situation

pristine – not changed by people; in its original state

refuge – a place of protection or shelter from danger or hardship

scales – one of the many small, hard, thin plates that cover fish, reptiles, and certain mammals

scientist – a person who does scientific research or solves scientific problems using scientific procedures, especially in the physical or natural sciences

scute – a bony plate; a large scale

submerge – to go or place under water

sympathetic – feeling or showing concern for someone in a bad situation

Enjoy this exciting excerpt from:

THE MYSTERY AT SHARK REEF

1

SHARK TALE

Avery looked through the jaws of a shark large enough to swallow her. Although she was an athletic cheerleader and a good swimmer, she was thankful she was at the

Palmetto Bluff Conservancy and not swimming in the ocean.

She and her **mischievous**, blonde-haired brother Evan were visiting their grandparents, Mimi and Papa, at their new home in Palmetto Bluff, South Carolina, near the coast of the Atlantic Ocean. Since their grandparents had recently moved here, they'd been like kids exploring the area. "They call this part of South Carolina the 'Lowcountry,'" Papa had said in his deep, booming voice.

Avery and Evan had groaned when Mimi, a famous mystery writer, said she and Papa were taking them to hear a lecture. "Haven't we just gotten out of school?" Avery had whined.

"Yeah," Evan had agreed, "we're on vacation. We don't want to learn *anything*!"

Mimi had clamped her hands firmly over her short blonde hair to cover her ears. "You know I've got funny ears," she said. "There are some things they refuse to hear. Besides, if you don't like this lecture, I promise I'll play one of those silly video games that you know I'll lose."

Mimi was right again, Evan thought, once he learned the lecture was on sharks. His mouth was open wider than the shark jaws his sister held. *I love sharks!*

"Guess I won't be beating you at a video game," he whispered to his grandmother.

"These massive jaws belong to a great white," a pretty young woman named Melanie Garcia explained. "They are lined with 300 triangular teeth that are set in rows. As you can see, these **serrated** teeth are perfect for ripping the flesh off the shark's prey. They can tear off chunks of flesh that weigh 20 or 30 pounds. One of a shark's favorite foods is seal."

Thank goodness it's not girls, Avery thought as she held the powerful-looking jaws.

Mrs. Garcia, a paleontologist with the University of South Carolina, held up the shiny white tooth of a great white shark in one hand. Then she held up a brown, heart-shaped tooth larger than her other hand. "This is the fossilized tooth of a **prehistoric** shark called megalodon," she said. "Its name means giant tooth. It swam in the world's oceans more than two million years ago."

"How about some more volunteers?" Mrs. Garcia asked, motioning for Mimi and Papa to join her at the front of the room. She opened a pair of cardboard jaws that had been propped against the wall and asked Mimi and Papa to step inside. The audience gasped.

"That shark could have swallowed Mimi and Papa in one gulp!" Evan exclaimed.

Avery giggled. She could just imagine Mimi walking around the inside of a shark in her favorite red high heels—she'd probably start decorating! And the cowboy hat that her tall Papa always wore would probably tickle the top of the shark's belly.

"The great white grows to an average length of 15 feet," Mrs. Garcia continued. "Megalodon grew to more than 50 feet. That's bigger than a school bus! In fact, it could have crushed a school bus in its jaws. It probably had the strongest bite of any animal that has ever lived. Its bite was even stronger than a Tyrannosaurus Rex dinosaur!"

"How do you know how long it was just by looking at its teeth?" Avery asked through the shark jaws.

"That's a great question!" Mrs. Garcia said. "We use a mathematical formula for that. We measure the length of one side of the tooth in inches and multiply it by ten. That gives us the approximate length of the shark in feet."

Evan was still impressed by the sight of his grandparents standing inside the massive jaws. "What did it eat?" he asked, hoping the answer wasn't grandparents.

"It's believed that the megalodons ate whales," Mrs. Garcia answered.

"Don't you have any real megalodon jaws?" another child asked.

"Shark skeletons are made of **cartilage**," Melanie explained. "That's like the stuff in your nose and ears."

Avery's face turned red. She had a feeling she knew what her silly brother was about to say. She had learned to expect it.

Evan snickered. "You mean boogers and wax?" he asked.

Mrs. Garcia laughed good-naturedly. "Guess I'll have to stop using that example," she said. "What I mean is that cartilage is very soft. It rarely fossilizes like bone. Finding an entire fossilized megalodon jaw would be very difficult. All that's usually found are the teeth."

"Where can you find **fossils**?" Avery asked, thinking she might start a new hobby.

"Believe it or not," Mrs. Garcia replied, "a man named Vitto Bertucci found one of the largest megalodon teeth ever discovered in a coastal riverbed right here in South Carolina! It was more than seven inches long. He was a jeweler who hunted fossils. It took Mr. Bertucci more than 20 years to find 182 teeth to place in a set of reconstructed megalodon jaws. They're 11 feet wide and nearly 9 feet tall. After he died, the set sold for more than $700,000!"

Everyone clapped after Mrs. Garcia thanked them for coming. "Before you leave, please take the time to look at all the fossils that are displayed," she added.

Evan and Avery made their way down the long tables filled with fossils. One tooth, tan and smooth, caused Evan to stop. He locked his hands and held them over the fossilized chomper. It was larger than both his hands put together. Near the top of the tooth he noticed a blackened area with a hole in it. "Guess this guy didn't floss," he said.

Evan hadn't seen Mrs. Garcia come up behind him. "You remind me of my son Noah," she said. "He thinks the same way that you do."

"Are these fossils valuable?" Avery asked Mrs. Garcia.

"They're all valuable," Mrs. Garcia said. "Some of them are priceless. But their value to me is not measured in money. It's measured in the stories they tell me about the past."

"What's your family doing for dinner tonight?" Mimi said, thinking that Avery and Evan might like to get to know someone their age who lived in the area. "We're taking Avery and Evan to one of our favorite cafés, Buffalo's. Maybe you could all join us."

"That sounds great," Mrs. Garcia said. "I'll call my husband to pick up Noah and meet us there. I just have to get all these fossils packed up first."

"Can we help?" Papa offered.

"Thanks," she said. "My assistant Sam will help. He's a graduate student in **paleontology**. He knows how to handle the fossils correctly."

Avery looked at the young man. He was thin with dark hair that fell to his shoulders and his clothes were rumpled, like he'd slept in them for days. He was talking to two men in the back of the room. While most of the people at the lecture had been parents and children dressed in casual shorts and flip-flops, these two men were wearing heavy boots. The boots were covered in a white dust that reminded Avery of baby powder. She watched Sam reach into his pocket before shaking hands with one of the men.

Avery had never even met Sam, but she had a strange feeling. Or maybe it was a hunch, like the characters in Mimi's mystery books often got when they met the bad guy.

There's something suspicious about this Sam character, she thought.

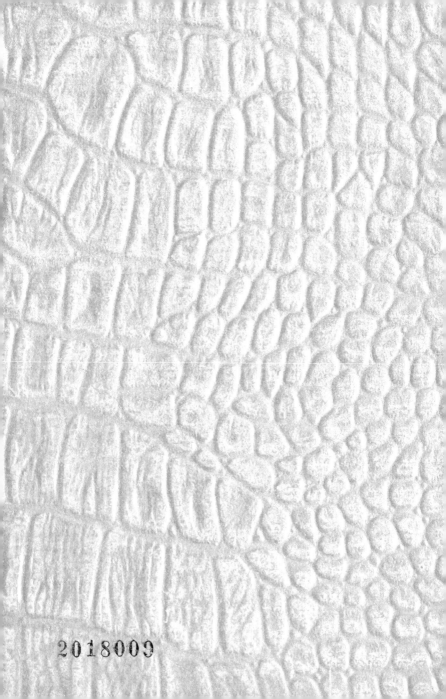

2018009

.